SESAME STREET
A GROWING-UP BOOK™

Too Little!

By Liza Alexander
Illustrated by Tom Brannon

A SESAME STREET/GOLDEN PRESS BOOK

Published by Western Publishing Company, Inc., in conjunction with Children's Television Workshop.

"What is Herry doing?" wondered his little sister, Flossie.

Herry rummaged around in his closet. Out tumbled his sleeping bag, air mattress, canteen, and tent.

"I'm getting ready for tomorrow night. My friend Hugo is sleeping over, and we're going to camp out in the backyard!"

"Oooh!" said Flossie. Flossie thought she'd like to camp out, too.

The next afternoon Herry was ready for Hugo. So was Flossie. She didn't have a sleeping bag, but she did have a quilt and a pillow. She didn't have a canteen, but she did have a special cup that belonged to Herry.

"Hi, Hugo!" said Herry. "Let's go out to the backyard!"

"Cowabunga!" said Hugo. Herry and Hugo rushed outdoors.

"Wait for me!" called Flossie as she ran after the big monsters.

The monsters pitched their tent. Flossie's daddy helped. Flossie tried to help, too. She fussed with the tent ties, but she couldn't tie a good knot.

"Here, Flossie," said Daddy. "Let me tie it for you. Now you kids scoot inside and help your mother while I light the coals. We're cooking out tonight!"

"Yaaaaay!" yelled Herry, Hugo, and Flossie, and they ran inside.

In the kitchen everybody was very busy. Mommy was making potato salad. Herry was patting the hamburger into flat round patties. Hugo was stirring up the monsterade. Flossie wanted to be busy, too, but nobody seemed to notice.

When it was time to go back outside, Flossie tried to
carry the pitcher of monsterade.

"Just a minute, dear," said Mommy. "I'd better take
that pitcher. You might spill."

Outside, Daddy was cooking at the barbecue.

"I want a double-chunky burger, please!" said Herry.

"Me too!" said Hugo.

"Coming right up, fellas," promised Daddy. He made Herry and Hugo each a big, scrumptious burger with all the fixings.

"Can I have a double-chunky burger, too?" asked Flossie.

"Honey," said Daddy, "your eyes are bigger than your stomach. You're really too little to eat one of the big burgers. I'll make you a little one."

After they had finished eating, it was still light
outside. Herry said, "Let's play monster in the middle!
C'mon, Flossie!"

But when Flossie was monster in the middle, the ball
soared back and forth above her head. No matter how
hard she jumped, her arms were just too short to reach
the ball!

"Time for marshmallows!" called Daddy. The boys found sticks and rushed over to the barbecue. Flossie found herself a perfect stick, but Daddy took it from her. He said, "Honey, you're too little to roast your own marshmallow. The coals are too hot. I'll roast it for you."

Even though the marshmallow was golden brown, just the way she liked it, Flossie did not think it was very delicious.

It was now dark. Flossie watched Hugo and Herry go into the tent. They turned on their flashlights and started whispering. "What are you guys saying?" called Flossie.

"We're telling ghost stories!" answered Herry.

"Can I hear the stories, too?" asked Flossie.

"Sorry," said Hugo. "Our stories are too scary for little monsters like you."

Then Mommy said, "Sweetie! What on earth are your pillow and quilt doing out here?"

Flossie scooped up the pillow, quilt, and special cup. "I need this stuff to sleep out in the tent."

"Flossie, dear," said Mommy, "the boys are sleeping out, not you. You're too little."

Flossie hurled Herry's cup to the ground. She
stomped her foot. She howled, "I'm too little for
everything!"

Then Flossie ran into the house and up to her room
as fast as she could.

Mommy followed Flossie up to her room. Mommy asked, "What's the matter, little one?"

"Don't call me that!" snapped Flossie. "I don't want to be little."

"Why not?" asked Mommy. "There are lots of good things about being little."

"Like what?" asked Flossie.

"Like bedtime stories," answered Mommy. "How about *Monsterella*?"

Monsterella was Flossie's favorite book. It was hard to resist. "Well, okay," said Flossie. Then she brightened up a bit.

Flossie felt much better when she woke up the next morning. Daddy was making pancakes! He let Flossie help. She cracked the egg for the batter and mixed it up.

Then Daddy let Flossie use the big wooden spoon to put some batter into the pan. "Look at the tiny bubbles on my pancake," said Flossie. "Pop-pop-pop!"

Then Daddy flipped Flossie's pancake for her.

When the pancakes were done, he put them on a plate. Flossie poured maple syrup on her pancakes and ate them all up!

All of a sudden it started to rain—very, very hard. All of a sudden two very, very wet monsters charged into the house.

Herry said, "Our tent collapsed!"

He and Hugo were soaked!

Flossie and Mommy ran to get towels and helped the boys dry their fur. Then Herry and Hugo went upstairs to change clothes.

After breakfast Herry and Hugo asked Flossie to play
hide-and-seek. Flossie was so little, she could squeeze
under a chair. It was almost impossible to find her.

Flossie helped set the table for lunch. Flossie knew just where to put the napkins and the forks. Then they ate Flossie's favorite: cucumber sandwiches.

After lunch Flossie was very sleepy. She felt too tired to climb the stairs to her own bed. Luckily, Flossie was still little enough to curl up in Daddy's lap and take a little nap.